The Yamas in Pajamas

A GUIDE TO YOGA FOR KIDS AND THEIR ADULTS

DEVEN SISLER

The Yamas in Pajamas

©2023 Deven Sisler

ISBN 978-1-66789-780-6

eBook ISBN 978-1-66789-781-3

TABLE OF CONTENTS

INTRODUCTION

What do you think of when you hear the word Yoga?

Many people think of yoga as those shapes you do with your body while breathing in a class with a bunch of other people. Some people worry that yoga is a religion that may distract their family from their core beliefs. And others think yoga is about being holier-than-thou-I-only-eat-kale-and-wear-tiny-yoga-pants. Yoga is about making shapes with your body while you breathe. It is also about being kind to yourself and to others, practicing honesty, and other wonderful principles that support you in being the most contented, confident, and peaceful version of yourself.

The yoga I practice and cover in this book is based on the eight limbs of yoga as written by the great sage named Patanjali. I use these principles of yoga to help me take care of the instruments of my body and mind. These principles also help me discover the sacred in the mundane or chaotic, peace in parenting, and maintain balance in all things I pursue. Practicing the eight limbs of yoga is not inherently influenced by an idea of God. You can use these principles as a system of daily living, a pathway towards your spirituality, or in support of your religion.

You do not need to eat anything in particular or wear anything in particular to practice yoga. Your body does not need to be a specific shape or size. You are here, and we can begin. Pause for a moment. Take a big inhale. Let that breath go.

Thank you for taking this time for yourself and for the kids in your life. Close your eyes for a moment, place one hand on your heart and one hand on your belly. Feel the miracle of your breath, your heart beat and send yourself three breaths of gratitude.

HOW TO USE THIS BOOK

Practicing yoga is an opportunity to explore yourself through awareness and it can hold great transformation for all of us. There is an abundance of books that cover the subject of the eight limbs of yoga for adults, and there is a growing wealth of wonderful books for children about how to get started with yoga, many of which focus on the benefit of practicing postures (Asana, the third limb) and breathing (Pranayama, the fourth limb). This book, however, is intended for adults who spend time with children, and offers a trail guide to begin exploring the first limb of yoga *for kids* so that together we may all access an inner wellspring of confidence and guidance towards contentment in modern times. When we explore the eight limbs of yoga as a whole, it can ignite transformation within and around us. You may be a parent who wants to bring more mindfulness into your living room or a counselor who wants to weave breathing techniques into your work. You may be an educator who wants to integrate mindful movement into your classroom, or a yoga teacher who wants to translate yoga into a kid's setting.

This unique offering, chock full of my personal research and time-tested techniques that work with all kids ages three to ten years old, draws from the full spectrum of yoga philosophy that is thousands of years old. It is intended as a guide, providing philosophical context for parents, caregivers, and kids yoga teachers who are interested in forging a path of co-learning with the next generation. In this book you will discover many techniques you can practice in your living room or classroom as part of your daily or morning routine. There are fun activities that make the esoteric tangible through journal prompts, guided meditations, and easy activities for kids and families. This text is not exhaustive, and I encourage you to find teachers on this path for deeper study. However, I hope it is a launching pad for your personal explorations.

Each chapter includes reflections, guided meditations, breathing exercises, journal prompts, some activities, and mindful movements or body shapes for each Yama, so kids and their adults can experientially explore these concepts.

- Guided meditations and breathing exercises can be used à la carte, or explored as part of the chapter in conjunction with other activities. If a child seems uncomfortable, frustrated or stressed by meditation, then consider stopping reading and come back to it another day.

- Journal prompts can be recorded in this book or you can get an unlined, blank journal to encourage creative expression – some kids like to write, others like to draw, and others may take this opportunity to write in spirals or upside down and backward. My intention is to provide a safe space for children and their personal reflections or intimate expressions. It is not an academic assignment, so they are free to respond how they prefer.

- During a class, workshop, or summer camp, I schedule "journal time" and make it very open. I recommend students include the date and may suggest writing prompts such as: "you can draw or write about what you are feeling" or "you can draw/write about anything we did today." Gently encourage them to record anything that was inspiring, motivating, or particularly frustrating.

- Mindful movement is moving with intention into the asanas or shapes we make with our bodies. The wonderful thing about the physical postures of yoga is each one has mental, physical, and subtle energy benefits. Even the sound of the names of poses in the Sanskrit language activates the parts of the body that are being engaged. I have included the Sanskrit name for each pose and invite you to try out the names as you practice the pose. Do not strive for or expect precision in alignment with children. I have included contraindications for these body shapes, so all generations of a family can try these movements with safety and awareness.

CHAPTER ONE:

WHAT ARE THE EIGHT LIMBS OF YOGA?

"Yoga is the uniting of consciousness in the heart.
United in the heart, consciousness is steadied, then
we abide in our true nature– joy."
~Nischala Devi Joy, The Secret Power of Yoga

Yoga is an ancient and scientific system of mindful living practices that can help each of us discover an internal wellspring of confidence, contentment, and peacefulness. It is about taking time to get to know your authentic, wonderful, and imperfectly perfect self. The practice of yoga entails essential philosophical tenets (the eight limbs of yoga from The Yoga Sutras), which include: ethical guidelines, making shapes with our bodies, breathing/energy control, and meditation. We most commonly think about yoga as concentrating on our breath while we put our bodies in different shapes or asana poses. These are the third and fourth limbs of yoga, and there is a great benefit to putting our full attention on this action, allowing the mind, body, and spirit to become fully present in the current moment. Less commonly thought of, but equally beneficial, are the six other limbs we can explore and unlock, leading to greater potential for transformation in self-consciousness and more joy in our lives. Yoga can be a physical practice, an ethical exploration, a scientific process of self-study, or a spiritual pursuit depending on the practitioner.

We can trace one of the roots of modern yoga to the writings of the sage Patanjali. Patanjali is referred to as the grandfather of yoga because he was the first to write down the thousands-year-old philosophy of yoga that was formerly only an oral tradition. This yoga is older than written words, and many people shared these concepts from voice to ear before they could be written down. These writings make up the "Yoga Sutras," which have subsequently been translated from the original Sanskrit, interpreted again and again, and shared on every continent of our planet. Each Sutra, or line of verse, is full of ancient history and inspiration. You can still find teachers who share this unbroken oral tradition, and it is recommended to find a teacher to continue studying the Yoga Sutras, or discourses, through interactive discussion for the deepest level of understanding.

Patanjali compiled the 196 Yoga Sutras, analyzed how we know what we know, and what causes us to suffer as humans. He then provided a set of guidelines for living a good life, eight limbs of yoga. The only physical shape referred to in the Sutras is a seated position. Can you believe it? Only one physical shape. All other shapes, or asanas, were added later in human history; therefore, it is essential that the physical shapes of yoga be practiced in conjunction with all the philosophical tenets in mind.

AN OUTLINE OF THE EIGHT LIMBS OF YOGA

1. Yamas (External Ethical Guidelines)

2. Niyamas (Internal Ethical Guidelines)

3. Asana (Postures or Body Shapes)

4. Pranayama (Breath & Energy Regulation)

5. Pratyahara (Withdrawal of senses)

6. Dharana (Concentration)

7. Dhyana (Absorption)

8. Samadhi (Integration: sustained coalescence (samapatti) of subject, object and perceiving itself)

The eight limbs are exciting, expansive, confusing, elusive, and inspiring, so in this book we will focus on exploring the Yamas. There are five Yamas or external guidelines. As Ravi Ravindra writes in The Wisdom of the Patanjali's Yoga Sutras, "The yamas are non-violation, truthfulness, non-stealing, containment, and non-grasping." How do we understand these concepts and make them accessible for kids? Let's explore!

The Yamas help us figure out how we can be with others in the world so we can be our most authentic self. We often think about behavior as good or bad, right or wrong, black or white. The world is more complicated and more beautiful than one or the other of these, and holds many more possibilities in between. These first five guidelines explore how self-control can help us moderate our own behavior so we can show up in our lives in the most peaceful, truthful, giving, and authentic ways possible. Let's discover what happens when we put the Yamas first in our practice of yoga.

CHAPTER TWO:

AHIMSA | NON-VIOLENCE OR PEACEFUL ACTION

O ften interpreted as non-violence, non-forcing, or peaceful action, Nischala Joy Devi interprets Ahimsa as "reverence, love, and compassion for all" in The Secret Power of Yoga. I find her interpretation well-suited for children, families, and anyone who works with children. Ahimsa is the foundation upon which our yoga practice and interaction with others is built. If we can try to act with peaceful action in each movement, each breath, and every word that we share, we create the possibility of abiding in peace and joy. The following pages explore techniques to introduce you to Ahimsa.

AFFIRMATIONS

An affirmation is a short phrase or word that we repeat. Whether we believe it or understand it fully or not, we trust that by saying this phrase or word out loud or silently that our subconscious and unconscious understanding will absorb the power of the words. Repeat this phrase out loud three times: "I am kind. I am peaceful. I like myself just the way I am." How does it feel to hear yourself say these words? Do you believe them? Keep saying them out loud, or silently until you do. You can return to your affirmation anytime you need courage, patience or support. Practice repeating them when you brush your teeth in the morning and evening each day this week and notice how you feel.

Use the chart below by filling in the days of the week and then checking off morning and evening when you practice this exercise.

DAILY AFFIRMATION CHART

Repeat out loud three times: "I am kind. I am peaceful. I like myself just the way I am."

Day of the week							
Morning							
Evening							

GUIDED MEDITATION | LOVING KINDNESS BODY SCAN

Practicing peaceful action is easier when you are feeling love for your body, mind, and spirit. The purpose of this meditation is to generate self-acceptance, love, and gratitude for yourself so you can be more peaceful in your actions. You can practice seated or lying down. It is preferable to do this meditation after a meal or a snack so you know the children are not hungry. Please note if any of the children that you are sharing this meditation with have atypical appendages, modify this text for them.

Close your eyes or keep them open, whichever will help you focus and relax. I will keep mine open and be watching the room to keep you safe. Place your attention on your feet. Think about all the places that your feet have taken you today. Are your feet in socks or shoes or not? Do they feel hot or cold? Think about how they got you here. They can move quickly or slowly. They can be loud or quiet. Send a silent thank you to your feet, without speaking, for taking you to all the places you want to go. PAUSE

Notice your hands. How do they feel right now? Think about all the doors your hands have opened today, all the things you have held, all the food and water your hands have brought to your mouth. Your hands help you get dressed, they feed you, they help you help your family clean up. They help you do all the things you want to do. Send a silent thank you in your mind, without speaking, to your hands for helping you do all the things you want to do. PAUSE

Place your hands on your ribs and listen for your breath coming in and out through your nose; feel your body being breathed. How do your hands feel on your ribs? Feel your breath filling the front, the sides, and the back of your ribs. Send a silent thank you to your lungs for filling you with fresh air whether you are awake or asleep. PAUSE

Now put one hand on your heart and one hand on your belly. Notice if there is any movement in your belly. Listen for any sounds your belly might be making. Think about all the food your belly digests and turns into energy for you to use every day. PAUSE

Notice if you can feel your heartbeat. Think about all the blood that pumps through your body from your heart to your brain to your belly to your muscles. This happens whether you think about it or not. Send a silent thank you to your belly, your brain, your lungs, and your heart for keeping you alive every single day without you ever asking. PAUSE

Notice how you feel right now. Is it any different than the beginning of the meditation? There is no right or wrong, good or bad, just noticing if you feel any differently. PAUSE

GUIDED MEDITATION | HAPPY, HEALTHY & PEACEFUL

This is one interpretation of the Tibetan Buddhist phrase, "Lokah Samasta Sukinoh Bhavantu." Please say these words out loud to accompany the guided meditation at home or in a non-secular environment. This guided meditation helps us cultivate the sweet sensation of connection with others and ourselves. As the adult facilitator or caregiver you can cue for the child group to repeat silently or out loud the following phrases.

Think of one person or animal who you love, any being. Choose the being that fills you up the most with warm feelings. Notice how you feel when you think of them. Then you can repeat this phrase, "May you be happy, healthy, and peaceful." Think about how it feels to wish this for someone else. PAUSE

Imagine your love for this being growing bigger and bigger. If any of the following cues make that feeling of love shrink at all, come back to the feeling of love you have for this first being. You could spend a whole year thinking about this love every day before you think about someone else, and that would be ok. PAUSE

Pretend that the person or animal that you love is standing in front of you. Imagine them saying to you, "May you be happy, healthy, and peaceful." Now you can repeat to yourself, "May I be happy, healthy, and peaceful." Imagine you can give each other a hug and feel your love for one another grow bigger. PAUSE

Now think of someone who is neutral to you. Neutral means you don't know if you like them or don't like them. They are just there–someone at the bus stop or at the library or the grocery store. Then you can repeat this phrase, "May you be happy, healthy, and peaceful." PAUSE

How do you feel when you send these words to someone you don't know?

Feel that love for the being you love, and feel their love for you grow a little bigger. Now think of all the people everywhere and repeat, "May all beings everywhere be healthy, happy, and free." How does it feel to think about all beings everywhere? PAUSE

JOURNAL | WRITING REFLECTION

For writing reflections, older students can be encouraged to write or draw their response, while younger kids can transcribe a letter that you write. These writing reflections can alternatively be used as discussion prompts with the family or in a class setting or put in an envelope and mailed off to the recipient.

Who do you love? Think about all the people and the animals that you love. Now you get to pick one. It could be a family member, a friend, a pet. Think about how much you love this being. Think of three reasons why you love them and write those in your journal. Notice how it feels to think about how much you love them. Write (or draw) a love letter to this being and let them know that you adore them.

_____

_____

_____

_____

_____

_____

_____

GUIDED MEDITATION:
ANGER TO LOVE FOR OLDER KIDS

"Darkness cannot drive out darkness; only light can do that.
Hate cannot drive out hate; only love can do that."
-Martin Luther King, Jr., 1963

Practicing Ahimsa, peaceful action, can be difficult when we are
feeling angry, frustrated, overwhelmed, sad or mad. The following
meditation is designed for older kids to investigate their anger and is
intended to help cool our anger.

Do you remember the last time you were angry? Why were you
angry? Where did you feel it in your body? Take a big breath in
and out, and notice where you felt it in your body. Did you clench
anywhere or want to hit something? Make sure the space you are
in is safe and clear. You can make tight fists and shake your hands
around and feel how angry you were for a few moments. Shake,
shake, shake your hands. Now open your hands, feel your soft
palms and imagine you can let go of that anger a little, teeny, tiny
bit. Breathe in through your nose and breathe out while sticking
out your tongue; let's do that again. This is called Lion's Breath. A
lion roars to warn others and protect its pride. Practicing Lion's
Breath can help us focus our anger into positive action. Let's do it
again and imagine letting go of a little more of that anger. PAUSE

Did you know your anger is always trying to tell you something?
Anger never walks alone. What is your anger trying to tell you?
And who is your anger walking with? Is it fear? Sadness? Injustice?
What does your anger want to tell you? Anger may tell you where
you are scared for someone or something and want to protect them.

Your anger may be covering up sadness or embarrassment. Anger may point to feeling powerless or overwhelmed against injustice. Notice what other feeling your anger is walking with and what it is trying to tell you. Breathe as you are feeling and ask yourself what you need to feel comforted or simply acknowledge and accept this other feeling. Your anger tells you something about who and how you love.

JOURNAL | SURPRISE

What do you love about yourself? List your top ten qualities (your favorite things about yourself) on a piece of paper. Then fold this up and hide it somewhere where you will surprise yourself with it on another day. Do you want to keep going? Write down ten things you love about someone in your family, fold up the paper, and put it somewhere that they will find it!

ASANA | BODY SHAPES

Table Pose | Bharmanasana

Benefits: Table pose, also known as hands and knees pose, is one of the most accessible poses. As humans, we all spent many months crawling in table pose which helped build our kneecaps, our body strength, and prepared us to stand, then walk. If you didn't crawl, it is a great practice to try. This is also the starting point to exploring spinal movement and sets up the transition to down dog or plank or child's pose. It builds awareness and prepares us for weight-bearing arm balances and inversions.

How: Place the hands and knees on the floor. Line the hands under or just in front of the shoulders, connect the whole palm on the ground, spread the fingers wide. Place knees directly under your hips. Toes can be pointed or flexed.

Common Contraindications: Recent or chronic wrist or knee injuries.

Variations:

- Wobbly arms or wrist pain: Lower to forearms to build strength
- Cow: Arch Spine, Inhale
- Cat: Hollow Spine, Exhale
- Fire Hydrant: Lift leg with a bent knee
- Balancing: Lift opposite arm and leg, reaching forward and backward

Mantra: "I am strong, kind, and peaceful."

Child's Pose (Little Mouse, Little Rock or Wisdom Pose) | *Balasana*

Benefits: Connecting the forehead to the earth can be very calming. It is a gentle stretch for the lower back. This is a primary resting pose. During the last month of gestation, this is the posture the baby body takes and allows our structure to properly develop so that we can relate to gravity when we leave that watery environment after birth.

How: Begin in table pose and bring the hips to heels and forehead to the earth.

Common Contraindications: Knee, ankle, or lower back pain.

Variations:

- Knee pain: place a folded blanket or towel under the back of the knee
- Ankle pain: flex the feet. You can also roll a blanket under the ankle
- Lower back pain: place two hands or a block under the forehead
- Stack hands to make a pillow for your forehead if it doesn't come to the ground

Mantra: "I breathe into my peaceful center."

Locust Pose | *Shalabhasana*

Benefits: An excellent back strengthener and opportunity to breath through the belly and connect with the support of the earth. Use this pose to warm up for other backbends and build postural strength.

How: Lie down with your forehead resting on the earth. Lift up the shoulders and reach the arms back Lift the toes, knees, and thighs up, your head off the mat. Breathe deeply into your lower belly to extend higher.

Common Contraindications: Shoulder, neck, or lower back pain or injury.

Variations:

- Arms back and behind
- Keep head hanging heavy to alleviate neck discomfort
- Press hands into the ground at your lower ribs to lift upper back without as much pressure
- Keep legs on the ground to avoid aggravating low back pain

Mantra: "I like getting to know myself."

CHAPTER THREE:

SATYA | HONESTY

Satya asks us to become truthful with ourselves and others, to become impeccably honest, and in doing so, to live to our highest integrity and potential. It is about recognizing, then speaking, your truth with precision and clarity. It is essential to visualize Satya nestled within Ahimsa as these first two Yamas are intrinsically intertwined. The loving-kindness of Peaceful Action keeps the truthfulness of Satya from becoming a harsh weapon.

When have you told someone a lie or a half-truth? I did it when I was younger because I was scared of the repercussions, like getting in trouble with my parents. We often choose the perceived safety of a lie over the fear of what the truth might bring.

I have a tendency to underestimate how long activities take, so in high school and college I was chronically late for classes, meetings, family gatherings, and friend dates. By overcommitting and underestimating, I was not being honest with myself and others about time. This chronic lateness led me to feel stressed, anxious, and worried that I was annoying others and almost caused me to be held back a grade in middle school. During my first yoga teacher training I started to realize how I was feeling and what I was missing out on by being chronically late. I made a conscientious effort to become more aware of time, to better prepare for each day and to invite space to be early rather than late. When we hold the hand of Satya we invite authenticity, accountability, and spaciousness over busyness.

In college, I longed for support from my parents for my chosen profession: acting. I doubted my talent and feared their response or disappointment, so I always told my family what I thought they wanted to hear instead of what was really in my heart. I became so good at telling others what I thought they wanted to hear that I lost a connection to my own hopes and dreams. When I learned to speak my truth, it helped me forge a confident career path that I continue to walk today.

Speaking your authentic, unique truth takes courage, compassion, self-awareness, and practice. For example, imagine your grandmother cooked you a delicious meal centered around mashed potatoes. Pretend you don't like mashed potatoes, even if you do. When she asks you how you are enjoying the meal, you might say three different things: "Oh, I like them!" because you don't want to hurt her feelings; or, "I really don't like this meal" because you want to be truthful; or, "I just can't stop thinking about the green beans you made last week" because you want to be truthful and kind. Honesty and kindness can go hand in hand.

Understanding honesty with kindness can be challenging at first, especially if we do not have a grasp on understanding our own emotions. When my older son was two, he could share that he was "happy" or "sad." Every nuanced emotion fell into one category or the other. Generally, most kindergarteners can name six major emotions: fear, anger, joy, sadness, disgust, and surprise. We can continue to grow our emotional vocabulary by actively naming and accepting our emotions.

JOURNAL EXERCISE

Each day this coming week notice how you are feeling and write down your feelings once in the morning, afternoon, and evening. At the end of the week journal about your experience and any observations you have. This seemingly simple act of labeling can increase your emotional intelligence, expand your understanding and enable you to communicate with honesty. You can accept our emotions by sharing or telling someone you trust how you feel. Another useful technique can be to write or draw how you feel in a journal.

FEELINGS CHART

Write one word or phrase about how you are feeling.

Day of the week						
Morning						
Afternoon						
Evening						

GUIDED MEDITATION | BIG BLUE SKY MEDITATION

This guided meditation/visualization is designed to give a visual metaphor to a common meditation phrase, "Imagine your mind is a big blue sky." This meditation practice could come after a body scan for an older group.

Close your eyes or keep them open, whichever helps you focus and relax during this meditation. Take a moment and observe—how does your mind feel? How does your body feel? What are your emotions right now? Whatever you are feeling is ok. Whatever YOU are feeling is ok. PAUSE

Notice your breath coming in and out through your nose. You can put your hand in front of your nose so you can feel your breath coming onto your hand. PAUSE

Rest your hands on your lap. You will have thoughts and you will notice sounds during this meditation, it's all ok. PAUSE

Pretend for a moment your mind is like the biggest, most vast blue sky you have ever seen or can imagine. How does it feel in your body to imagine that? PAUSE

Now some clouds float in. These clouds are similar to the thoughts in your mind or emotions in your body. What kind of clouds cover your mindscape? Are they little skinny ones, big flat fluffy thunder clouds, or are they like a big blanket of cotton covering the sky, or something else? What do your clouds look like? PAUSE

Whatever clouds you imagine are OK, and no matter what, we always know the sky is blue and clear on the other side of the clouds. PAUSE

Imagine you can put your thoughts in the clouds and a little bit of wind sweeps them away, so you just keep coming back to watching the sky of your mind. As a thought comes into your mind, put it in the cloud let it float on by. LONG PAUSE

Just as the clouds are something in the sky, not the sky itself, you are not your thoughts or your emotions. Your mind is always blue and vast like the sky so keep coming back to your breath as it sweeps your thoughts and clouds away. PAUSE

MANTRA

Om is a sound that can mark the beginning and ending of any yoga practice. *Om* is an indivisible seed syllable, an essential sound that can be neither defined nor broken down. The repetition of this sound, called mantra in Sanskrit, can help focus the mind, freeing it from distractions and bringing clarity so we can be more present, just as it is in this moment.

Repeat the sound of "om," or "a-u-m," and listen to the silence after the "m". Repeat this eight times and observe how you feel in your mind, your body, and your emotions. Repeating the sound of om with your own voice, as loud or as quiet as you like, can be an anchor to feeling safe and present in this moment. The repetition of this mantra can disrupt the negative, less helpful pathways of thought in your brain.

"OM SHANTI SHANTI SHANTI"

Pronounced "a-u-m, sh-an-tee, sh-an-tee, sh-an-tee". The sound of m centers us, and shanti translates from Sanskrit as peace. When I repeat this phrase, I touch my forehead with my thumbs and hope that there will be peace in my thoughts, then I touch my lips and hope there will be peace in my words, and finally, I touch my sternum and hope there will be peace in my heart and actions.

GUIDED MEDITATION: FEAR TO SAFETY

"Fear keeps us focused on the past or worried about the future.
If we can acknowledge our fear, we can realize that right
now we are okay. Right now, today we are still alive,
and our bodies are working marvelously"
—Thich Naht Hahn

Can you remember a time when you were a little bit scared of something from a book or your imagination, or from last Halloween? Try to pick a memory for this exercise that has just a little bit of scary, not too much. It is best to pick something that was pretend or imaginary. If this exercise becomes overwhelming, tell a trusted adult and ask for help. Now, remember this small scary thing. Where did you feel this feeling in your body? Take a big breath in and out and notice where you felt it in your body. How did it feel? Imagine your hands have strong protective armor on them that can protect you and keep you safe from anything. Place your strong protective hands on the place in your body where you feel afraid. Now feel your feet on the ground. Could anything make the small scary thing silly? A funny nose, googly eyes, or too big sparkly shoes? Can you transform the tiny scary thing into something silly or funny that makes you giggle? Can you feel afraid and laugh at the same time?

Now pretend your fear is your friend and just needs you to be its buddy. What is your fear asking you? What does your fear need you to do to feel safe? Build a blanket fort? How can you be a good friend to your feeling of fear? Journal about or draw what your fear needs to help it feel safe.

JOURNAL

"I have learned over the years that when one's mind is made up, this diminishes fear; knowing what must be done does away with fear."
—Rosa Parks

Write about a time when it was difficult to tell the truth. Why was it hard? Why is it important? What did you want to say? Who was the person you could tell? Why did you trust them?

If you haven't told this person that they helped you tell the truth, take a few minutes and write them a thank you note letting them know you trust them and they help you stay strong when the truth feels hard.

_____

_____

_____

_____

_____

_____

_____

_____

ASANA | BODY SHAPES

Anjali Mudra | *Palms Together Pose*

Benefits: As babies gain control of their upper limbs, their ability to bring their hands to meet at the midline and move symmetrically is one of the most essential developmental patterns. This fundamental movement sets the foundation for crawling. Bringing the left and right hands together and finding our sense of midline is a physical metaphor for our ability to find our unique center and inward focus.

How: Bring the palms of your left and right hands together at your sternum. Repeat the sound of "om" or "om shanti" here and notice how you feel.

Mountain Pose | *Tadasana*

Benefits: This pose is the structural foundation for all the standing poses. From Mountain pose, we build awareness of how to properly stand on our feet. The steady, stable foundation of this pose builds an efficient neutral posture for standing and can bring awareness to inefficient habits.

How: Touch your big toes together or keep your feet hip-width apart, feel the bottom of your feet. Rock forward and back then side to side on your feet to look for the center of your standing posture. Can you push down through the front, back, and both sides of your feet? Imagine each bone in your spine stacking one on top of the other and a little string pulling your head up towards the sky.

Variation: If someone cannot stand, follow the cues in a seated position.

Partner Poses:

- Stand back to back with a partner, feel the warmth of their back. When you both lean back into each other, you also receive more support for your own ability to stand. Tune into your own breath and your partner's. Can you match them?

- Group Tadasana: Stand in a line or a circle shoulder to shoulder to imagine yourselves as a beautiful mountain range.

Mantra: "My base is strong and steady. I stand peaceful no matter the season or weather." OR "I am a mountain strong and steady. I am ready for anything."

Visualization: Imagine you are a mountain; what kind of mountain would you be?

Horse Stance | *Utkata Konasana*

Benefits: This is a pose seen through many different training lineages, such as martial arts, Tai Chi, and Shadow Yoga. It mobilizes the hips/knees/ankles while increasing muscle tone and strength through the legs or foundation. Holding this pose for one to two breaths longer, when you start to feel discomfort to help develop mental fortitude, perseverance, and endurance.

Common Contraindications: Knee injury/pain, groin strain.

How: Start in a wide-legged stance, draw the heels in, turn the toes out, and sink your hips as parallel to the ground as you can while keeping the knees over the ankles. Reach your arms out to the side.

Mantra: "I can rest in the strength of my legs. I am stronger than I can imagine"

Tree Pose | *Vrksasana*

Benefits: Tree pose builds strength and proprioceptive awareness. Proprioception is your ability to know where your body is in space, how you move, and how to balance. Sometimes it is referred to as our "sixth sense." This pose also builds flexibility in the hip of the lifted leg and can improve your ability to balance.

Common Contraindications: Ankle or hip injury/strain, shoulder injury.

How: Stand with your feet underneath your hips. Shift your weight onto one leg, lift the other, bend the knee out to the side, and place your foot on the inside of your balancing leg above or below the knee. Your hands can stay together and reach to the sky. Steady your gaze on an unmoving space or object.

Partner Pose: Stand in a line or a circle shoulder to shoulder, then take your hands to your neighbors' shoulders (or kids to adult waists), lift one leg and imagine yourselves as a grove of trees communicating underground from root to root.

Mantra: "My roots are deep. My trunk is strong. My branches lift up towards the sun. I can bend with the wind, but I do not break."

Visualization: Imagine you are a tree; what kind of tree would you be? Would you have spring flowers, fall leaves, pine needles, or simple winter branches?

Game: "Trees in the Wind" – divide the group in two. One half is in tree pose while the other half moves around them like the wind, making noises and movements to try to distract their concentration. Be sure to specify no touching as one of "the wind's" rules.

CHAPTER FOUR:
ASTEYA | RECIPROCITY & GRATITUDE

Asteya is classically translated as non-stealing, but it can be looked at as reciprocity and gratitude. It is the feeling or recognition that, in everything, there is enough, and with enoughness there is an inspiration to give back. These are the concepts we can look at with kindness and curiosity in our lives. In contrast, jealousy and stealing are the opposing forces of Asteya. When we focus our attention on appreciating or being grateful for all the gifts we currently have, rather than being distracted by that which we don't have, we can increase overall happiness and decrease stress, anxiety, and depression.

JOURNAL

When are you jealous? How does it feel in your body, mind, and emotions when you are focused on jealousy? I can feel jealous when I spend too much time on social media, and I compare my life to the perfect snapshots from other people's lives. I forget that these are just one picture or short video from their lives and not the whole picture of their struggles and reality. I can lose self-confidence and feel less inspired when I am in a jealousy spiral. Does this sound familiar? One way I can combat this is to limit my time on social media. It can be hard to turn off my device, but I try to remember this quote when I do: "Breathing in, I know I am breathing in. Breathing out, I know I am breathing out. Breathing in, I calm my body and mind. Breathing out, I smile," by Thich Nhat Hahn. What can you do about your relationship with jealousy? Can you invite any curiosity?

Try this Journal Practice by just noticing how you feel after different activities. Make it a practice to write down a few words without any filter or judgment, and then look at the end of the week to see if there are any patterns.

HOW I FEEL — ACTIVITIES CHART

Write down a few words without any filter or judgment after each activity.

Day of the week							
After yoga or meditation							
After a walk outside							
After tv or social media or gaming							

GRATITUDE JOURNAL

For the next week write three things in your journal that you are grateful for, as well as how you are feeling each day. At the end of the week, reflect by reading your journal for the week, observe how you feel and your general disposition.

DAILY GRATITUDE LIST

Day of the Week	Three Things Morning	Three Things Evening

ACTIVITY

When was the last time you received a gift? Who was it from? Did you say thank you or write a little thank you note? Draw a thank you card for this person in your life. A thank you note or drawing is a special way to show that we appreciate the act or gift we were given.

MANTRA: SO HUM

Find a comfortable sitting position and rest your hands on your lap. Repeat the sounds "so hum" eight times. Notice how you feel before you know the translation of these words.

"So hum" mantra can translate to "I am that. I am enough." The sentence "I am that" refers to you as a precious being in the vast, magical universe. You are the universe, and the universe is you! "I am enough" is just that. You are perfectly imperfect, wonderful and unique, exactly how you are in this very moment. Whenever you need a reminder about how amazing you are, repeat this mantra for eight repetitions every day this week. Journal about how you feel before and after you practice this mantra.

ANCESTOR JOURNAL

Who are your ancestors? Your ancestors are the grandparents of your parents, or anyone who came before you in your family. If you don't know their names, ask someone in your family who might. There are many different kinds of family, so your family tree may include adoption, divorce and remarriage, or connections that are love binding and not legal or blood. You may come across family members who you don't always agree with or ancestors who don't share your values. Remember, the first Yama is Ahimsa so you may ask with loving curiosity as to why they are the way they are. You can ask the Universe for forgiveness on their behalf. You can ask your parents what they remember most fondly about their grandparents and one lesson they learned from them. Write a letter to your ancestor who has passed on, thanking them for their lesson that is being handed down today.

_____

_____

_____

_____

_____

_____

_____

_____

JOURNAL

"In our every deliberation, we must consider the impact of our decisions on the next seven generations."
~The Great Law of the Iroquois Confederacy

Pretend for a few minutes that you are a great-great-grandparent, and you get to talk to your great-great-grandchildren. What would you want to tell them? What do you want them to remember about your life? What lesson would you like to give to them? What is one thing you want them to remember about how you left the world for them? What do you want them to remember that you gave back to your family and the planet in your lifetime?

_____

_____

_____

_____

_____

_____

_____

GUIDED MEDITATION | TAPROOT

This guided meditation/visualization is designed to help you get grounded and centered. This could come after a body scan, or before a gratitude meditation for a group with established concentration and focus.

Different plants and trees have different kinds of roots. You can close your eyes or keep them open, whichever helps you feel safe, relaxed, and focused on the visualization. I am going to keep mine open.

Today, we are going to think about and visualize a taproot. It is a large, central, dominant root in a plant that grows directly downward. It can be very strong and very thick, like a carrot, beet, sweet potato, or radish. Some trees can rely on their taproot for centuries. Think of the tallest pine tree you can imagine or you have seen. Notice how high it reaches up into the sky—its taproot goes as deep into the dirt, the bedrock, the earth, as it grows tall. PAUSE

Whether you are sitting on the ground or in a chair, notice where you are connected to the floor, the earth. Feel the places where your body touches the ground. Feel your spine grow taller towards the sky. PAUSE

As you breathe in, imagine energy running towards the top of your head. As you breathe out, imagine energy running back down your spine. PAUSE

Pretend you can see a root of energy growing down through the floor and sinking into the dirt. This is your taproot, your central grounding connection to strength. PAUSE

As you breathe in, feel energy coming up from the earth, the bedrock, the dirt into your taproot, up into your body, and into your lungs/heart/brain. LONG PAUSE

As you breathe out, imagine your taproot growing longer and deeper into the earth. PAUSE

With every breath in, you can imagine energy coming up, nourishing you from the earth. PAUSE

With every breath out, you can imagine your thoughts, energy, and taproot grounding down towards the earth's core. PAUSE

ASANA | BODY SHAPES
Happy Baby Pose | *Ananda Balasana*

Benefits: Just as a baby discovers its feet for the first time, we can bring a joyful curiosity to our yoga exploration. Happy Baby Pose offers a gentle hip opener and can help release tension in the lower back.

Common Contraindications: Hip Flexor strain/injury.

How: Lie on your back, stretch your legs into the air. Take the outer edge of each foot in a hand and let your knees bend towards your armpits.

Variations:

- Tight hips/legs: Use a strap to reach the feet
- To go deeper: Straighten one leg at a time.

Mantra: "I am open and fluid."

Pigeon | *Kapotasana*

Benefits: Pigeon pose can help release tension in outer external rotators, can counteract the negative effects of chair sitting, and can create a sense of internal space. After a good warm up, you may encourage longer holds so that gravity may help elongate the muscles being stretched.

Common Contraindications: Knee pain or surgery, hip flexor/psoas strain.

How: From downward dog, take your right knee to your right wrist and settle the shin as parallel to the front of your mat as possible. Flex your toes, keep your back leg long, and root your hands by your hips to lift your torso, shoulders, and head.

Variations:

- Knee pain/injury/replacement—supine pigeon (lying on your back)

- Alleviate hip strain—place a bolster or blanket underneath the hips

- Stronger core version—arms can reach up

- Deeper relaxation—fold forward over the front leg and place your forehead on a block

Mantra: "I am calm in the midst of storms, raging seas and wild winds. I am calm."

Visualization: Imagine you are a bird. What kind of nest would you build? How would you nestle down to sleep each evening with the sunset? How would you wake up every morning with the sunrise?

Crow | *Bakasana*

Benefits: Crow can be one of the most accessible arm balances and a gateway to practicing strong handstands. It establishes control in the fingers, connection and engagement of the core, and demands firm commitment. It builds confidence and is an exciting, inspiring exploration.

Common Contraindications: Wrist, shoulder, elbow, strain or injury.

How: Start in a deep squat and place the knees as far up the inner tricep as possible. Place both palms and all your fingers on the earth. Tip forward to pour weight into the arms as you lift up through the torso. Levitate both toes off the earth.

Variations:

- Wrist, shoulder, elbow, strain or injury—Supine Crow (a core workout on your back)
- Stronger core version—work towards straightening the arms
- Side Crow

Mantra: "I lift up and fly."

42

CHAPTER FIVE:

BRAHMACHARYA | ABSTAINING FROM EXCESS

Excess can be anything from too much time on devices, too much candy, too much work, too much sleep or staying up too late, or even too much yoga. Brahmacharya asks that we find balance and moderation in all things that we do so we can savor each moment and revel in our individual, imperfectly perfect "enoughness." There is a subtle and profound perspective change when we realize that everything and anything can be taken too far from indulgence into excess. Social media, television, sweet treats, work, and sleeping in—are particular things that can be good when in balance, but too much creates imbalance. The concept of Brahmacharya helps us discover what balance is and enjoy the sacred sweetness of moderation.

We can wear our busyness and pack "to-do lists" like a badge of honor. Yet, when we examine this compulsion to pack everything into the limited time of every day and week, we can invite stress, worry about getting it all done, and miss the beautiful unplanned, unfilled moments.

Imagine how you would feel if you didn't need to change anything, fix anything, or accomplish anything to be "just right" in this body in your life in this moment. Just imagine how you might feel. I have two young children who don't want me to change anything. They love me unconditionally, and they simply want more of my undistracted attention. They want me to be present with them. I am perfect as I am for my family, and when I can recognize this, the mundane becomes sacred.

BREATH EXPLORATION

Notice your breath coming in through your nostrils and out through your nostrils. If this exercise becomes stressful, overwhelming, or frustrating, return to your normal breathing pattern. As you breathe in, fill up as much as you can, fill up a little more, hold for a moment, and then let it go when you need to. Breathe normally for a moment and notice how you felt when you were holding your breath. Your lungs tell your brain that your breath is full and that you need to let it go, to breathe out, to be able to breathe in again. We can't possess our breath in because we need to find balance between in and out. We need them both. Count the length of your breath in and then match it with the length of your breath out. If your in is 1-2-3, match your out to 1-2-3. Notice your inhale and your outhale. PAUSE After a few more breaths, notice if you can lengthen and deepen the breath in and out, or if you want to repeat the steady counting. There is no right or wrong answer, just noticing. Maybe 1-2-3-4, 1-2-3-4. Again, if this exercise feels uncomfortable, return to the lower number or your normal breath pattern.

This exercise invites an overall sense of balance to the mind, body, and emotions.

JOURNAL

Have you ever stayed up too late? Or spent too much time watching television? Or too many hours playing a video game? Pick one time in particular and try to remember how it felt in your body, your eyes, your head? Do you remember how your mind and thoughts handled that too-muchness? What were your feelings? If you can't remember how it felt for you, do you remember how it was to be with a friend, a parent, or a sibling after they stayed up too late? How long did it take you (or them) to recover?

_____

_____

_____

_____

_____

_____

_____

_____

_____

SELF-AWARENESS EXERCISE FOR OLDER KIDS

Material: A square piece of paper and colored pencils

Directions: Fold each paper into quarters and crease. Unfold and trace the edges of the quarters, so the paper has four boxes. Label each box with the following: School/Afterschool; Me Time; Friends/Family; Sleep. Write all the activities that you do on an average day, like last Tuesday, in the corresponding box and include approximately how many hours. School/after school can include extracurriculars, homework, a job, and sports. Me Time can include self-care like brushing teeth, reading for fun, drawing, any activity that you do by yourself when you are not sleeping.

School/Afterschool	Me Time
Friends/Family	Sleep

Can you notice, through the lens of Brahmacharya, if things are balanced in your week as you reflect on this exercise? Notice what you are in control of and if there is anything that can change to invite more balance.

BEFRIEND YOURSELF ACTIVITY

"What I like doing best is Nothing."
"How do you do Nothing?"
asked Pooh after he had wondered for a long time.
"Well, it's when people call out at you just as you're going off to do
it, 'What are you going to do, Christopher Robin?' and you say, 'Oh,
Nothing,' and then you go and do it.
It means just going along, listening to all the things you can't hear,
and not bothering."
"Oh!" said Pooh."
—A.A. Milne, Winnie-the-Pooh

Schedule time this week to be alone inside, for at least fifteen minutes, or outside in a safe place. This is a very important date that you are scheduling with yourself and by yourself. Leave all televisions, devices, books, and distractions someplace else. Tell your family that you are having some alone time, and ask that they respect that by leaving you alone! You can bring paper and pen or pencil. Think about the Winnie the Pooh quote and explore what it means to "do nothing." At the end of your scheduled time, journal about the experience by yourself. Write about any uncomfortable thoughts or feelings, and see if you can befriend any loneliness or boredom that come up too!

ASANA | BODY SHAPES
Low Lunge/Dragon Pose | *Anjaneyasana*

Benefits: Lunge poses increase muscle tone in the legs and build overall stamina. They also prepare the upper leg and lower torso for back bending and front splits. This builds proprioceptive awareness, our awareness of where the body is in space, because we cannot see the back leg.

Common Contraindications: Toe or knee injury for low lunge.

How: Start in tadasana with the feet hip-width apart, step one foot back and place the flexed toes and one knee on the ground. Bend your front knee and reach your arms into the sky for low lunge. Push off the back toes and lift the back leg for the more powerful version of high lunge.

Visualization: "My arms become wings, as I lift them up they fill with wind. As I lower them I stick out my dragon tongue and roar." What color are your dragon wings?

Warrior 3 or Airplane Pose | *Virabhadrasana III*

Benefits: In this pose, you build confidence in your ability to balance the whole body on one leg. It strengthens the muscles in the outside of the standing leg and builds a stronger core connection to midline in the rest of the body.

Common Contraindications: Outer hip or glute strain/injury.

How: From High Lunge Pose, tip forward onto the front leg while lifting the back leg. Keep the hip closed/parallel to the ground to maximize the benefits of this pose. Arms stay at your side, and you can look down (for a plank version) or forward and up for a little upper back-back bend. Switch to the other side. Play with the position of your arms.

Group Pose: Stand in a circle in mountain or tree pose, place hands on shoulders or waists of your neighbors and send one leg back and behind you for this "Skydiver variation."

Mantra: "I balance and take flight."

Half Moon Pose | *Ardha Chandrasana*

Benefits: Half moon can be a difficult balancing pose that tones the muscles of both legs. It increases strength in the front, back, and sides of the torso while building proprioceptive and vestibular awareness in the whole body. The presence of a "dark side" in the unseen back body can help build mental endurance and a sense of self-compassion through practice.

Common Contraindications: Hip flexor/external rotator strain.

The "how to" with this pose varies by age:

- Ages 4-8: Start with your back at the wall, line up the edge of one foot with the wall. Tip forward until that side hand touches the ground with your bum and back resting on the wall. Reach the other hand towards the ceiling.

- Ages 9+: Start in Triangle pose and place your back hand on your hip, lean your weight onto the front foot as you lift your back leg. Stack your top hip over your bottom. Optionally, reach your back arm up to the sky. Switch arms.

Mantra: "I reflect the love that surrounds me."

CHAPTER SIX:

APARIGRAHA | NON-HOARDING, NOT BEING ACQUISITIVE

Aparigraha can be a complicated concept to explore, so remember that every Yama still nests in the loving embrace of Ahimsa, and be kind to yourself as you are learning new things. Aparigraha is about letting go, allowing space for imperfection, and not taking more than you need. Our society and media try to convince us that we "need" a lot of things to be happy– these shoes to run the best, this cream for your skin, this outfit for this season, and this special toy for the most fun. Aparigraha is about letting go of the obstacles that are holding us back as well as not getting too attached to that which we do like. Stuff can be a big obstacle, as what we own also owns us. Plastic was invented in 1907 and before that everyone, everywhere, mostly reused, mended, or traded the things they had over and over again. Today, many people buy new things and throw away things when they don't feel like they "need" them anymore, and this cycle is filling up trash dumps all over the world and starting to choke our oceans.

For my neighbors' birthday, instead of asking for gifts they put out a bunch of toys and books that they loved but stopped using on a table. On the birthday invite, they asked everyone to bring a book or toy that they love and would like to give away. At the party guests would give the item that they brought, and take one that the birthday kid gave. Everyone ended up with something new and no new plastic was purchased. Can you pick five or ten toys, books, or things in your room that you don't need anymore and give them away as useful gifts to someone else?

NATURE WALK EXPLORATION

Go on a nature walk and, while outside, look for a special object in nature. When you return to your home or classroom, share what you like about your object. Then pick a special place in the room to put your objects for everyone to enjoy. You can hold this object when you practice breathing exercises or meditation, and then return it to its special place.

GUIDED MEDITATION | FALLING LEAVES

This guided meditation/visualization is designed to help you feel connected to our planet and identify with seasonal aspects of deciduous trees.

Sitting, lying down, or standing up, imagine you are a tree with leaves in the summer. Imagine in your mind's eye what kind of tree you would be and in what season. Pretend you can feel your roots growing down into the soil and deep into the earth receiving water, nutrients, and messages from other trees there. Feel the power from the earth coming into the tendrils of your roots, up into your trunk, and giving you life. Reach your branches up into the sky to receive rain, sunlight, and carbon dioxide. Notice the green greenness of your leaves. PAUSE

The weather begins to change and get cooler. The nights get longer, the days get shorter. Watch the color of your leaves begin to change, too. See them fade from green to reds-yellows-oranges. PAUSE

One day, a big gust of wind comes, and the tree lets go of each and every leaf. They are swept into the brilliant blue sky above and fall into a pile on the earth. In your imagination to pretend you are the happiest kid who gets to jump into this beautiful pile. Take your leap, then lie down in the cozy pile of autumn leaves. Look up at the bare tree that has let go of each and every leaf without holding on at all. Notice your exhale, and let go of your breath as the trees let go of the leaves. PAUSE Let go. Let go. PAUSE

BREATH MEDITATION

Notice your breath coming into your nose and leaving your nose. The breath in is called an inhalation, the breath is called an exhalation. We have to let air out to be able to breathe in. Focus your attention on your exhalation. Before we go on, remember you can always return to your normal breath if you feel stress, frustration, or anxiety. Listen to what your body needs to do. Can you extend, lengthen, or deepen your exhalation? Can you breathe out a little more deeply? To help focus your attention on your breath out make a soft "*shhhh*" sound. Use your fingers to help you count to ten repetitions of a longer exhale. How do you feel after you focus on the breathing exercise?

This exercise can help slow down the heart rate, increase a sense of calm, and help the nervous system relax. This is not true for everyone, so listen and notice how you react.

LETTING GO EXERCISE

When we can start letting go of stuff, or the hold our things have on us, we have more space for connection with other people we love and more time for ourselves. This week get a box and fill it with clothes or toys and things you use the least. As you pick up an object, say thank you to it for being useful, bringing you joy, or keeping you warm. When you have filled the box as much as you can, then label it with the date and put it in a closet. Write on your calendar or ask an adult to set a reminder for two weeks from now. In two weeks' time notice if you can remember what is in the box. If not, give it away. If you do remember what is in the box then give it away with purpose to a friend or younger family member.

PASS IT ALONG ACTIVITY

Sit in a circle with your family or yoga class. Pick an object that is interesting (a shell, a ball, meditation globe, or electric candle) and pass this coveted object around the circle one person at a time. Everyone can have an opportunity to say one thing they like about the object while everyone else listens. Then we pass it along until everyone has had a turn.

ASANA | BODY SHAPES

Bridge Pose | *Setu Bandha Sarvangasana*

Benefits: Bridge is a wonderful backbend that strengthens the back body while gently stretching the front of the body.

Common Contraindications: Spinal herniation, back injury or sciatica.

How: Begin lying down on your back and bend your legs to press your feet firmly into the floor. Lift your hips towards the sky. Keep your head in line with your neck and keep pressing down into your feet, shoulders, and arms as you lift your belly. Imagine a stream flowing underneath your body.

Mantra: "I let my breath and love of life flow."

Legs Up the Wall or Waterfall Pose | *Viparita Karani*

Benefits: This is one of the most gentle and relaxing inversions. It allows blood to flow from the feet and legs back through the major veins and into the heart, giving this muscle a semblance of rest.

Common Contraindications: High/Low Blood Pressure.

How: Start seated close to a wall, roll onto one side and then walk your feet up the wall. Scoot your hips as close to the wall as is comfortable.

Variations:

- Place a bolster underneath the hips for more supportive relaxation
- For tight hamstrings—set up farther away from the wall
- For an inner leg stretch—take a wide straddle

THE YAMAS IN PAJAMAS

Partner Pose: Adults set up into waterfall pose, kids can pretend to be a "rock" in the waterfall, a "frog" jumping and resting or a little fish swimming and resting.

Mantra: "I am fluid and flowing."

Resting Pose/Corpse Pose | *Savasana*

Benefits: This is considered by many scholars and yogis to be the most important of all the yoga poses. During this time, we invite complete relaxation of the body, stillness, and silence by creating a cozy atmosphere. The rest during the end of the yoga class allows the breath, movement, and overall learning to integrate into the cells, muscles, nervous system, organs, and emotions. The purpose is to let go of movement, thought, focus on the breath, and just be. This is not a nap time or opportunity to fall asleep, although that sometimes happens.

Common Contraindications: Inability to get down onto the ground.

How: Lie down on your back. Stretch hands and feet to the air and shake off any leftover movement, then bring them back to rest, palms facing up. Close your eyes and rest.

Variations:

- Constructive Rest—place the bottom of the feet on the ground with knees bent This variation allows the spine to be neutral and the craniosacral fluid to flow naturally.

- Bolster or blanket under the knees

- Frog on a Log—place a rolled-up blanket or bolster directly underneath the spine supporting the head. Allow the arms to open out to the side, which will give a gentle stretch to the pectoral muscles.

- Burrito—everybody rolls his or her self up in a yoga mat or in a blanket on a yoga mat

- Eye Pillows—place eye pillows

- Guided Relaxation or Yoga Nidra

Partner Poses:

Lizard on an Alligator – Adults lie face down on their tummies. Kids can rest on top. Encourage kids to be still and not wake their hungry alligators.

Super Burrito—the whole family can lie down on one side of a blanket, then roll up, surrounded by the blanket for a cozy, quiet time.

Mantra: "I am able to rest and be still. My hands are still, my feet are still, my eyes are still, my voice rests."

Visualization: I melt into the ground like ice melting into a pool of water. My body is heavy and supported, like a still pond or a lake.

NOTES: *Turn music to very calm or off, turn the lights down very low or off. Lower your voice to guide students to the ground, lying on their backs for a classic savasana. They can close their eyes or keep them open. Set realistic expectations, savasana may be one to two minutes with younger children. Provide enough vocal guidance and structure so children better understand how to rest without falling asleep, while offering as little stimulation as possible.*

CONCLUSION

Take a moment to find your most comfortable seat, and place one hand on your heart and one hand on your belly. Take a few deep breaths. Can you recall the moment you first picked up this book? Think back over the journey of reading it and notice what you have learned about yourself, about this human experience of being in the world and having a breathing, thinking, feeling body.

By completing this book you are commencing on a journey of continued investigation of yourself and how you live in community with others. This is an ideal time to look for a teacher if you don't have one already. My first experience with the Yamas was to read about, then memorize, the translations during my first yoga teacher training. Since then, I have returned year after year for decades to continue this cyclical exploration of these concepts.

They help me calibrate my inner compass towards living my most authentic life with as much compassion, honesty, reciprocity, balance, and non-attachment as possible. Welcome to the community of self-investigators, compassion researchers, and grace givers. We are honored and grateful to have you in this community.

RECOMMENDED READING

Winnie The Pooh by A.A.Milne

The Little Frog Awakes by Eline Snel

Peace is Every Step by Thich Naht Hahn

The Yamas & Niyamas by Deborah Adele

The Secret Power of Yoga by Nischala Devi Joy

The Wisdom of Patanjali's Yoga Sutras by Ravi Ravindra

ACKNOWLEDGMENTS

I extend my deepest gratitude to all my teachers and all their teachers who have inspired this work for kids and their adults, may we create a more peaceful world through these teachings. There will always be a special place in my heart for those who supported me teaching kids yoga while folding in contemplative thought at the beginning of my career: Jennifer Brilliant, Kevin & Erin Maile O'Keefe. Jennifer Yarro for embodying how to connect mindful movement and philosophy. Jenny Sauer-Klein for your mentorship as a teacher and entrepreneur. Chris Loebsack for being my mentor, co-teacher, and cheerleader. Janet Stone for moving me through the Yamas in my pajamas surrounded by laundry. Suzie Newcome for your support, organization, and encouragement. Kelli Mae Willis for supportive, collaborative, and inspiring co-teaching, motherhood, and community. To my mother in law, Lisa Tauxe, for your dedicated commitment to learning and your contribution for the title of this book. To my editors: Sophie, Crystal, and Britta for your knowledge of commas, eye for detail, and appreciation for the written word. And above all else, my supportive parents, encouraging sisters, fabulous friends, inspiring husband, my children's gracious grandparents, and my unconditionally loving children— thank you from the depths of my heart for loving me as I am.